A Story from West Africa

Vacation in the Village

by Pierre Yves Njeng

Boyds Mills Press

Published by Caroline House
Boyds Mills Press, Inc.
A Highlights Company
815 Church Street
Honesdale, Pennsylvania 18431
Printed in China

Publisher Cataloging-in-Publication Data
Njeng, Pierre Yves.
Vacation in the village / by Pierre Yves Njeng.
—1st American ed.
[32]p. : col. ill. ; cm.
Originally published : Yaoundé, Cameroon :
Editions AKOMA MBA, 1996.
Summary : A boy discovers and takes pride in the customs of his
people when he visits his family's village.
ISBN 1-56397-768-0 (hc.)
ISBN 1-56397-823-7 (pbk.)
1. Cameroon—Social life and customs—Juvenile fiction.
I. Title.
[E]—dc21 1999 AC CIP
Library of Congress Catalog Card Number 99-61827

First edition, 10000
Book cover designed by Randall Llewellyn
The text of this book is set in Usherwood Book.

(hc.) 10 9 8 7 6 5 4
(pbk.) 10 9 8 7 6 5 4 3 2

So that all the children of Africa,
like birds smitten with delight,
may follow the thread of the dream to its end—
and to Marie Wabbes

My name is Nwemb, and Ngo Nwemb is my little sister. Every morning I have to tell her, "Quick! Drink your milk. It's seven o'clock, and we'll be late for school." But one day I was even more impatient.

It was the last day of school. Mother left work early and came to pick us up at the end of the day. She congratulated us both on our excellent report cards.

After dinner, Father announced that we were going to spend our vacation in a village outside the city. My sister was happy all evening long. Me, I was worried because I'd never been to a village.

I didn't know anyone in the village I could have fun with. I couldn't even take all my toys with me. I wondered if children were allowed to play in that place.

In the morning we arrived at the train station at the last minute. My father ran to buy the tickets, and we picked out a compartment on the train.

We were leaving the city, and all my friends were staying behind. I knew I was going to be bored in the village. The train pulled out, and I fell asleep.

When the train stopped at the village, I woke up to the shouts of the vendors running along the station platform. My father helped us off the train. He let me carry my own bag.

It was heavy, and I was happy that a boy named Masso helped me. He was my age, and he knew my grandparents well.

My grandparents were happy when they saw us. Grandfather got out of

his armchair, and I threw myself into his arms. He hugged me tight.

Masso stayed to help me get settled, and my grandfather told

me that Masso and I were related. That evening we had dinner together.

We ate a lot that first night, my sister and I. There was hare and manioc, and orange juice to drink. It was quite late the next morning when Mother woke us up.

I watched my father work on rebuilding the top of the well so the children couldn't fall in. My grandmother gathered our clothes to wash.

Later in the afternoon Masso told me all he had done that day. I was excited at the idea that soon I could go with him into the forest.

In the evening Grandfather told us stories about the forest. He also told us about the customs of our courageous ancestors. During the night I dreamt about them.

The next day my mother let me go fishing with Masso, but the fish ignored our hooks. We didn't catch anything. We were both tired.

On the way back, Masso caught a turtle. He gave it to me to show his friendship. I was thrilled. We named it Kulas.

The days went by, each filled with discoveries. Kulas joined in all our games. Masso taught me how to make things out of bamboo.

Some days, as we hunted in the fields, Masso and I tracked easy prey. I was very proud to have him as a friend. Thanks to him, my village vacation had become magical.

I was completely happy. Soon I knew every inch of the forest. I could even climb trees, and in the evenings we would fall under the spell of Grandfather's voice lulling us with his stories.

The end of vacation came too soon. I was sad because I had grown to love the simple village life. I let Masso have all my books. I took Kulas back to the city. But I know I shall return to the village one day soon.